vity
Book

By Melinda Long

Illustrated by
David Shannon

Houghton Mifflin Harcourt
Boston New York 2010

So you want to be a Pirate?

Shiver me timbers!
'Tis not an easy task ahead!

FIRST, ye need to know how to look like a pirate—hat, eye patch, and teeth as green as the beautiful sea (peg leg optional!). Then ye have to learn to walk and talk like a pirate. Ye have to say "Aargh!" and "Ahoy." No "please" or "thank you," unless ye want to walk the plank! And don't ye forget: a pirate's got to be prepared. What do ye know about treasure maps and sea chanteys? Aargh! 'Tis time to learn!

AYE, lads and lasses, life on the open seas with yer mates is the best—the ole Jolly Roger flapping in the sea breeze and the smell of a freshly swabbed deck!

ARE ye ready for the challenge? Then off ye be! Smartly! Thar be rough waters ahead, but, aye, thar be treasure too!

The first thing ye need, laddie,
is a spiffy pirate hat!

How to Make a **Pirate Hat**

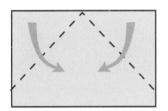

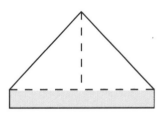

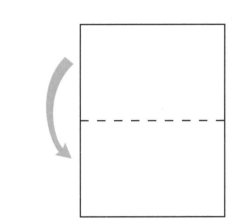

Instructions

1. Fold a 1/2 sheet of newspaper in half from top to bottom.

2. With the creased edge at the top, fold the top right corner and the top left corner until the two corners meet on the paper (there should be extra space below where they meet).

3. Using the extra paper below the two corners, fold up the front piece to create a one-inch strip that covers the two corners (paper may need to be folded one or more times, depending on the size of the paper left). Secure edges with tape.

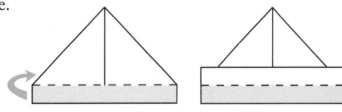

4. Turn the hat over and repeat step 3 for the back piece.

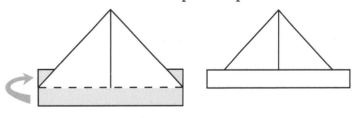

5. Decorate the hat using your favorite art supplies (crayons, markers, stickers, glitter).

How to Make an Eye Patch

Materials

1 piece of cardboard • Pencil
Scissors • Stapler
Markers or paint • String
Hole punch • Glue

Aye, matey, make sure to
ask an adult for help!

Instructions

1. Draw the shape of your eye patch on the piece of cardboard. Make the shape a little larger than needed; it can be trimmed down.

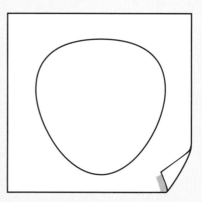

2. Using the scissors, cut out the shape that you made on the cardboard. Hold the eye patch up to the wearer to check for size. If necessary, trim the eye patch down.

3. To make the eye patch more comfortable for the wearer, use the scissors to cut a slit from the bottom to the middle of the patch. Take the cut edges, overlap them a little, and staple them together.

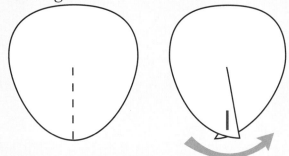

4. Color the eye patch with either a black marker or paint. If using paint, set the eye patch aside to let the paint dry thoroughly. Color your eye patch any color you want (maybe green to match your teeth!). Use stickers, glitter, or more paint to decorate your eye patch.

5. Using a hole punch, create holes on the left and right side of the eye patch.

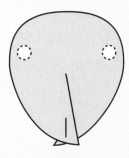

6. Measure the length of the string so it fits comfortably around the wearer's head. Tie the string to each hole.

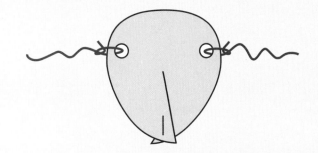

7. Your eye patch should be ready! Try it on and give a big hearty "Aargh!"

Now that ye have yer hat and eye patch,
yer on yer way to becoming a pirate.
Draw a picture of yerself in full pirate garb.

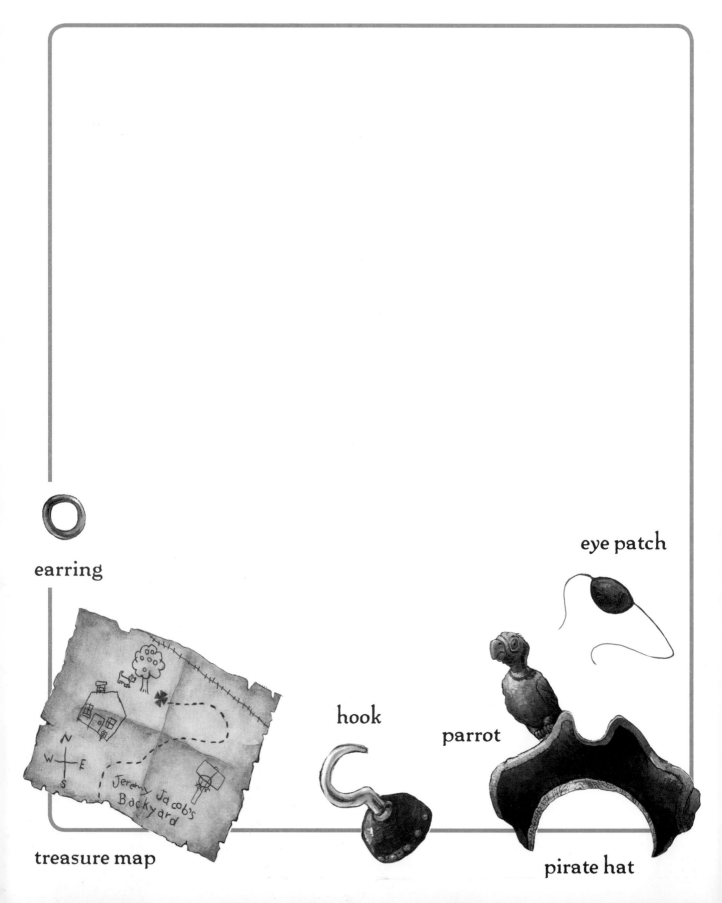

earring

eye patch

hook

parrot

treasure map

pirate hat

Why Pirates Don't Teach Manners

SNEEZING: The proper way to sneeze, laddie, is to warn yer mates when you feel a bit of the nose tickle coming on. "Duck and cover, ye filthy scoundrels! I'm gonna blow!" Then ye take a deep breath and blow like yer fillin' the ship's sails: "ACHOO!" And remember, a pirate's sleeve makes the best hankie.

Treasure Hunt

Help the pirates find the buried treasure!

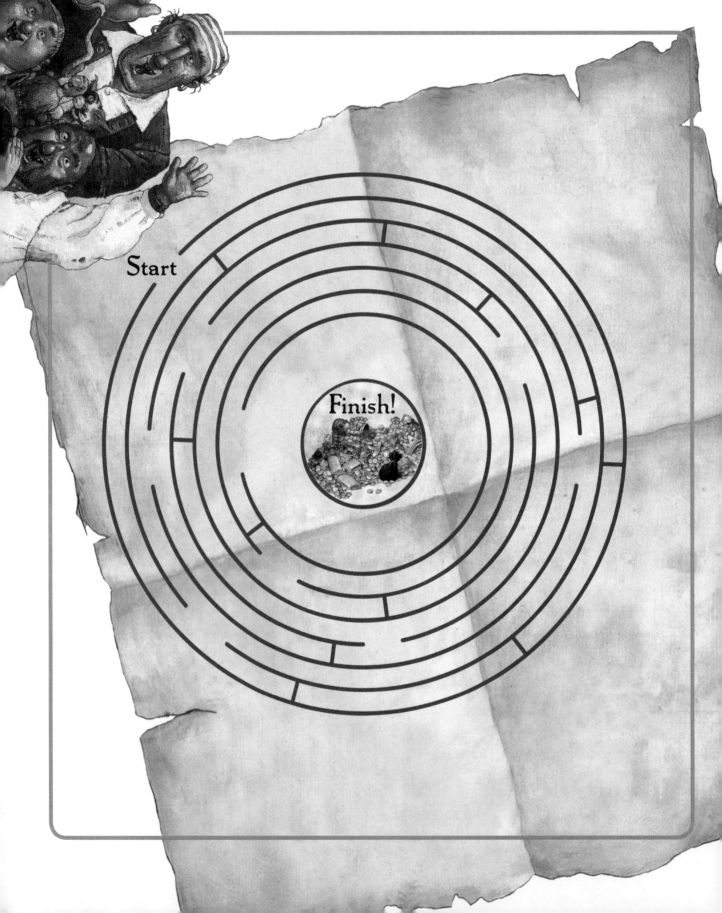

Start

Finish!

One sunny day, the pirate captain _____ and his
Pirate name

crew set sail on a search for treasure. With their island destination
visible through the captain's _____, a wave of excitement
Pirate tool

washed over the crew. The closer their ship got, though, the more
sharks they noticed swimming around the tiny island.

"_____! We'll never get past them sharks, captain,"
Expression of surprise!

exclaimed one of the pirates.

"I've got me sights set on a beautiful treasure. We've got to get 'round
those beasts. If ye got yer doubts, then maybe you'd like to walk the

_____!"
Part of a ship

Not wanting to become a quick and easy feast, the pirate crew
prepared the rowboat.

While the _____ flapped in the breeze, the crew rowed their
Pirate flag

way toward danger.

Just as they found themselves in the heart of shark territory the
captain shouted, "Belay there! Have any of you scurvy dogs seen me
treasure map?"

The crew looked around the small rowboat with no luck.

Just then a big shark swam by with the map clenched in its jaws.

"_____! I guess the sharks will get to keep me
Expression of frustration

treasure . . . for now."

Complete the Picture

Sing a Sea Chantey

A pirate's got to know a chantey or two. Aye, it keeps the crew happy. Sing this song as loud as ye like! Loud enough so they can hear ye an ocean away!

I'm a pirate, a pirate I be
I live my life on the open sea
A parrot on my shoulder, my only company
A pirate's life is the life for me

I have green teeth and a wooden peg
It comes in handy when I make scrambled eggs
I take what I want and don't need to beg
Aye, except to the shark that stole me leg

I'm a pirate, a pirate I be
I live my life on the open sea
A parrot on my shoulder,
my only company
A pirate's life is the life for me

Set sail for the nearest island coast
A chest full of treasure is what I seek most
Rubies and emeralds and diamonds to boast
A mountain of gold to take back to me post

I'm a pirate, a pirate I be
I live my life on the open sea
A parrot on my shoulder, my only company
A pirate's life is the life for me!

Now that you've had a little practice with this chantey,
try writing the next stanza or, if yer up to the challenge,
write yer own chantey for yer crew to sing.

Make Yer Own
Treasure Chest

Every pirate has a bit of treasure and needs a place to put it!

Materials
Shoe box
Paper to cover box
Markers, crayons, or stickers
Treasure

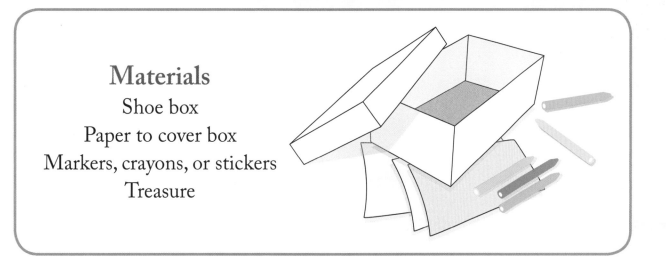

Instructions

1. Find an empty shoe box and cover the lid and the bottom of the box, separately, with paper.

2. Use markers, crayons, or stickers to decorate your treasure chest.

3. Place your treasure inside the box (maybe gold doubloons!).

4. Hide the treasure chest where other pirates won't be able to find it!

Aye
Yes

Ahoy!
A way to say hello or
grab someone's attention

Blimey!
An expression
of frustration

Belay
Stop

Gangway!
Yelled to clear a
passage in a
crowd of pirates

Jolly Roger
A black flag with
a white skull and
crossbones

Matey
A friendly term
used to address
another pirate

Smartly
Quickly

Talk
Like a Pirate

It's important to choose yer
words wisely, or ye might find
yerself walkin' the plank!

Landlubber
A person who
lives on land

Walk the plank
Be forced by other
pirates (hopefully
not yer own crew!)
to walk off a plank
on the side of the ship
and into the deep ocean

Shiver me timbers!
An expression
of surprise

Me hearties
My fellow crewmates

AARGH!

How many words can ye make out of the letters in
"SHIVER ME TIMBERS"?

_____

_____

_____

_____

_____

_____

_____

_____

Complete the Picture

What do the pirates see?

Why Pirates Don't Teach Manners

EATING: Grab as much of the grub as ye can before yer mates have a chance. "Outta me way, ye scallywags!" Ye won't be needing any spoons or forks. Just grab the grub with yer paws and eat. When the food is in yer belly, don't forget to swab yer plate clean with yer tongue. Ye don't want to miss a bit of sauce! 'Tis the best way to wash yer dish as well.

Create Yer Own
Pirate Flag

Ye can fly more than just the Jolly Roger at the top of yer mast! Pirates often have their own flags so other ships can easily identify the ship's captain. Use the space above to create yer own pirate flag.

Cannonball!

Instructions for Cannonball! card game (plays like Snap)

1. Deal all 36 cards. Place your stack of cards facedown on the table in front of you.

2. On your turn, take the top card of your pack and place it face-up in a new pile in the center of the table.

3. If two cards in a row are the same, yell: "CANNONBALL!" and place your hand on the pile. Take all the cards in the pile. Add these cards to the bottom of your main stack of cards (facedown).

4. If you call out "CANNONBALL!" at the same time as someone else, the person with their hand at the bottom of the pile is the one who gets the cards.

5. If you call out "CANNONBALL!" by mistake, you must place all your unturned cards in the center of the table.

6. The winner is the player who collects all of the cards!

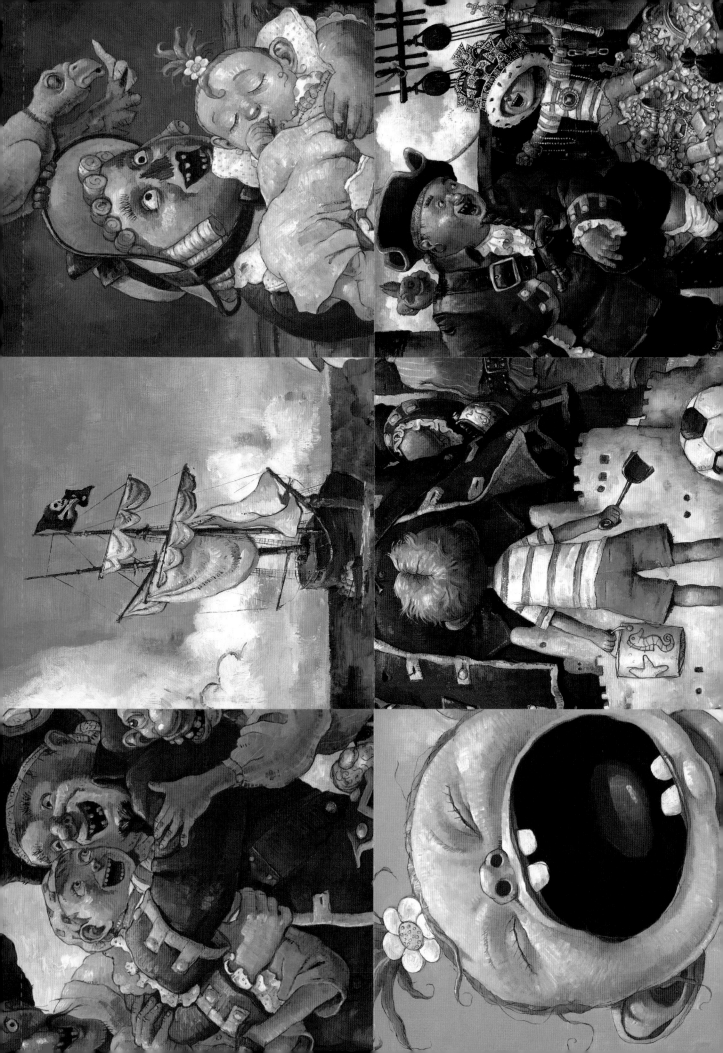

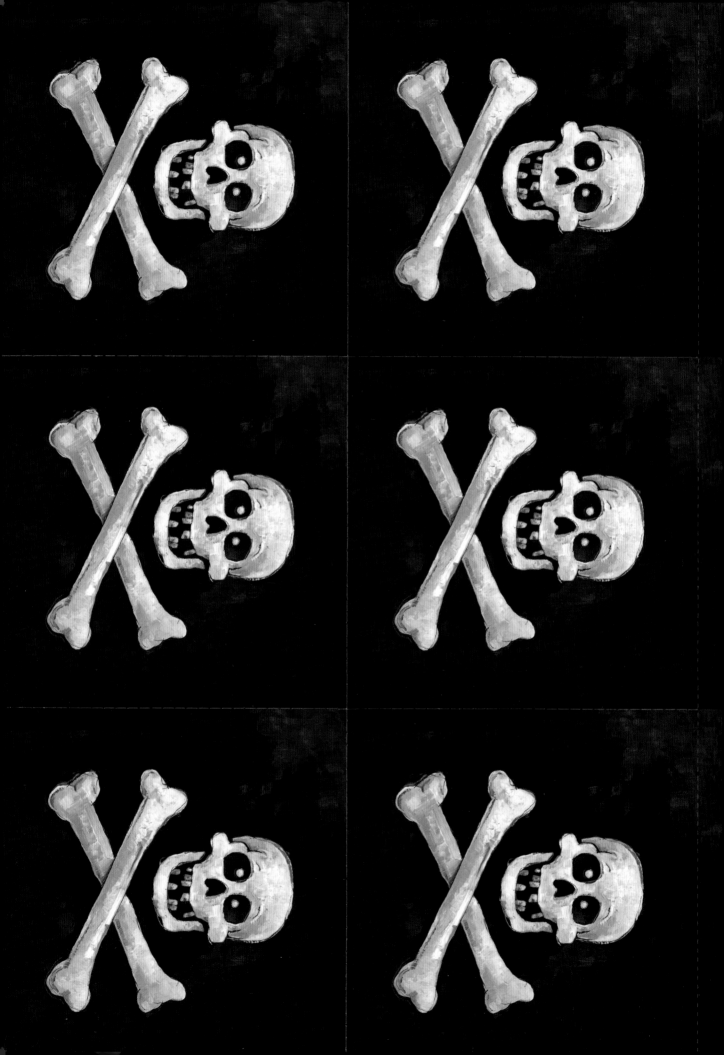

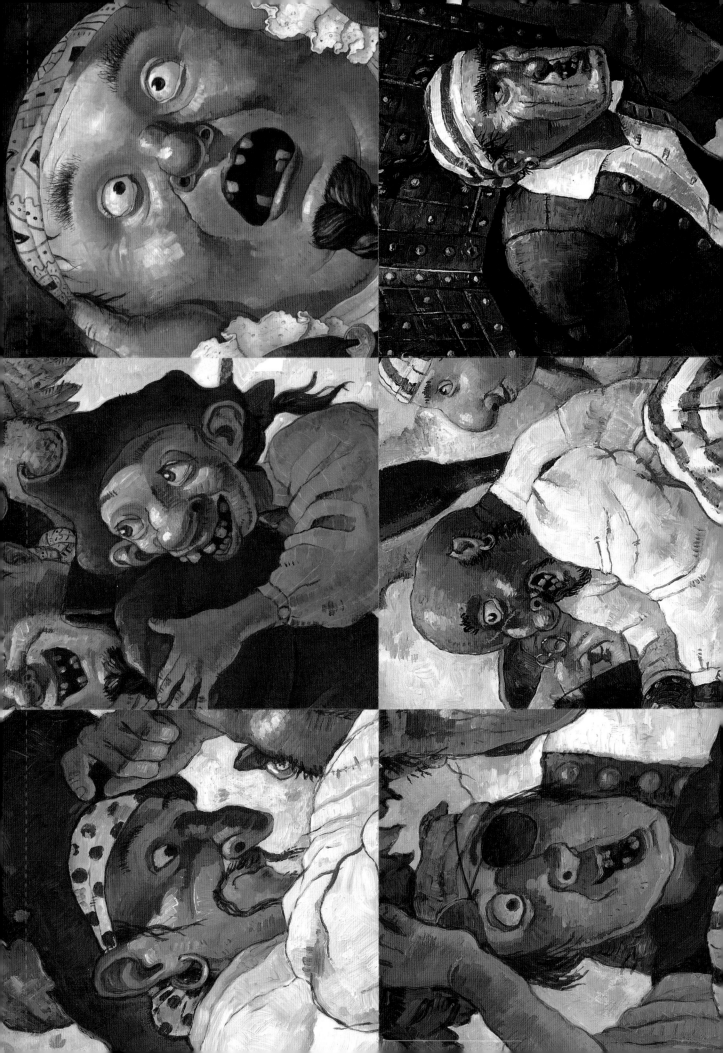

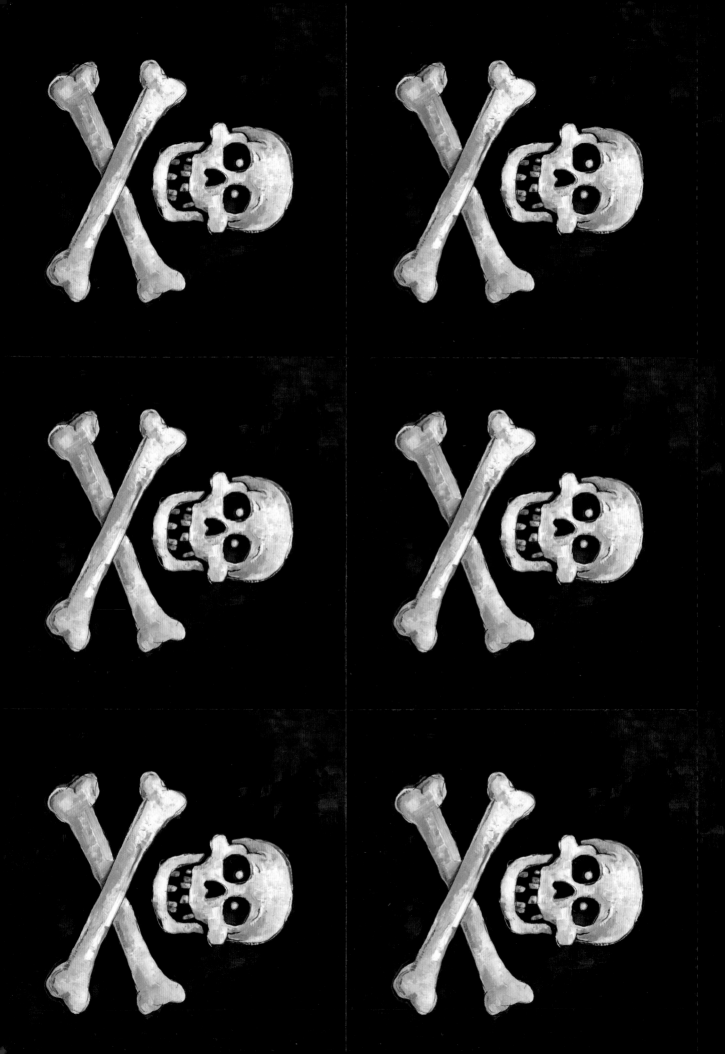

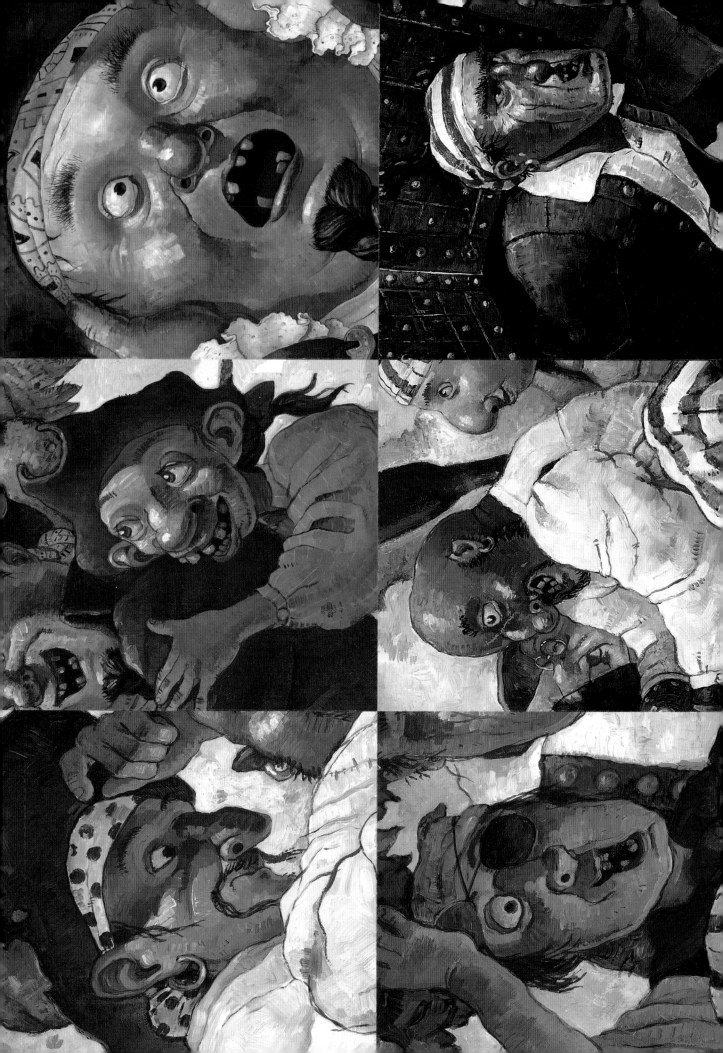

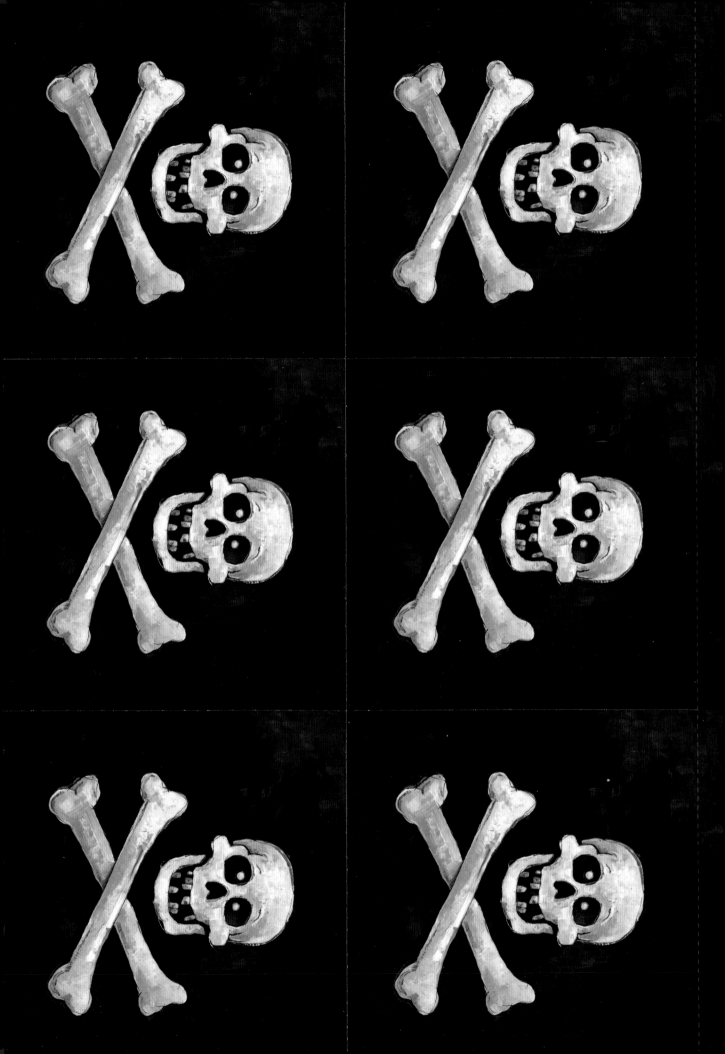

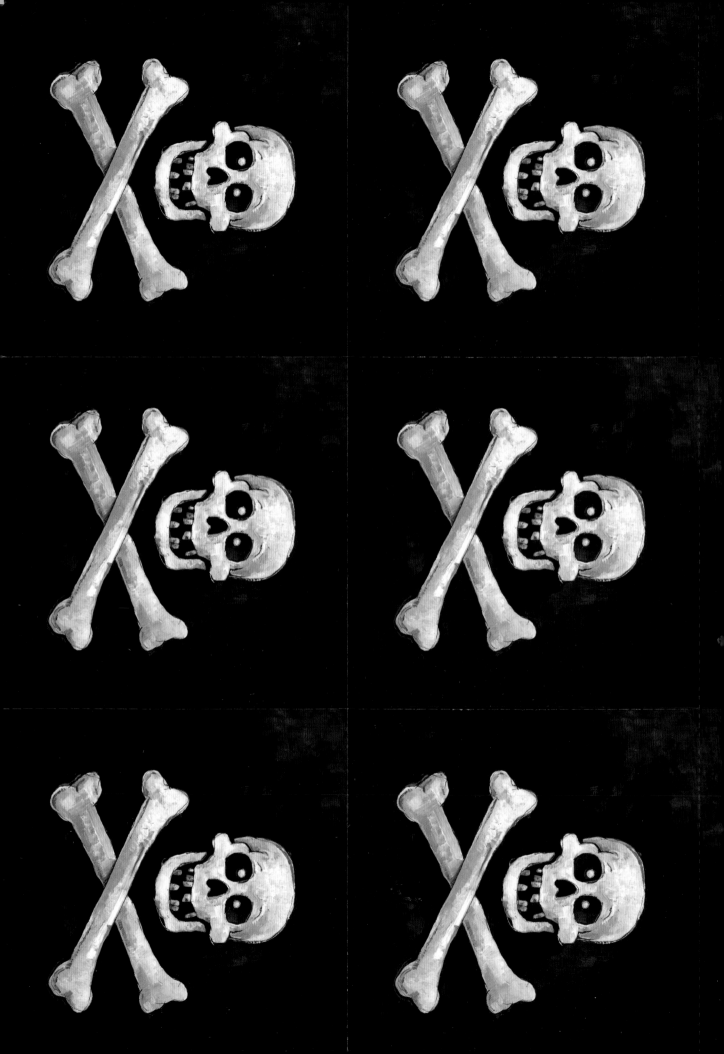

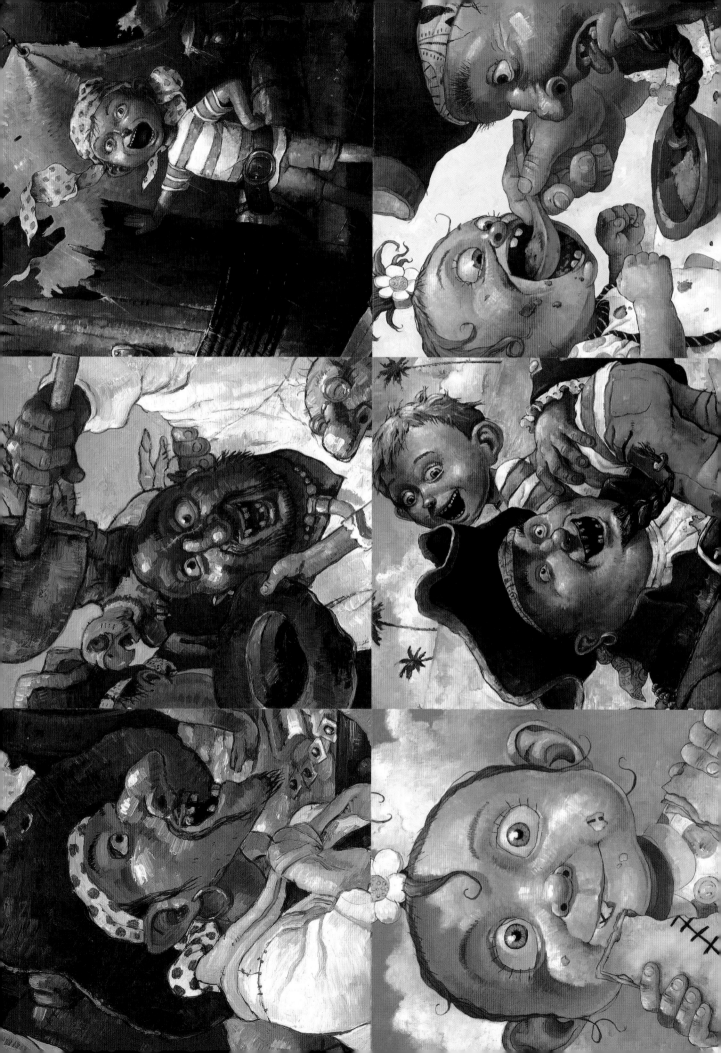

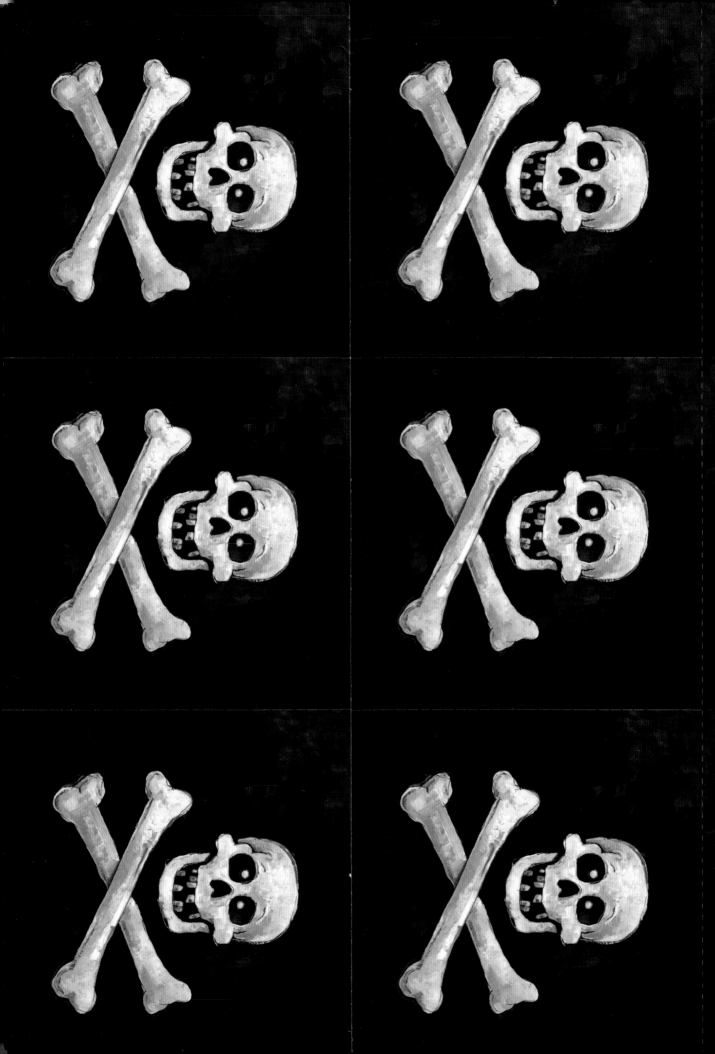